NO ROOM IN THE INN

and Other Stories from *A Midnight Clear*

KATHERINE PATERSON

LODESTAR BOOKS

Dutton   *New York*

Copyright © 1995 by Minna Murra, Inc.

Library of Congress Cataloging-in-Publication Data
Paterson, Katherine.
A midnight clear : stories for the Christmas season /
Katherine Paterson.
p. cm.
Contents: A midnight clear—Merit badges—Watchman, tell us of
the night—A stubborn sweetness—No room in the inn—Poor
little innocent lamb—In the desert, a highway—Star lady—
Amazing grace—Exultate jubilate—The handmaid of the Lord—My
name is Joseph.
ISBN 0-525-67529-9 (alk. paper)
1. Christmas—Juvenile fiction. 2. Children's stories, American.
[1. Christmas—Fiction. 2. Short stories.] I. Title.
PZ7.P273Mi 1995
[Fic]—dc20 95-12590
CIP AC

Published in the United States by Lodestar Books,
an affiliate of Dutton Children's Books,
a division of Penguin Books USA Inc.,
375 Hudson Street, New York, New York 10014

Published simultaneously in Canada by McClelland & Stewart, Toronto

Editor: Virginia Buckley
Printed in the U.S.A.   First Edition   10 9 8 7 6 5 4 3 2 1

Reprinted by arrangement with Lodestar Books.
an affiliate of Dutton Children's Books.
a division of Penguin Books USA Inc.

for all the saints
of
Lafayette Presbyterian Church
Norfolk, Virginia
and
First Presbyterian Church
Barre, Vermont
with gratitude and love

Still through the cloven skies they come,
With peaceful wings unfurled;
And still their heavenly music floats
O'er all the weary world;
Above its sad and lowly plains
They bend on hovering wing:
And ever o'er its Babel sounds
The blessed angels sing.

"It Came Upon the Midnight Clear"
Edmund Hamilton Sears, 1810–1876

Contents

A Midnight Clear

IN THE MIDDLE of the algebra test, Jeff saw the cloud for the first time. He couldn't make heads or tails of the fifth problem, so he did as he usually did when he was stuck: He looked out of the window. That was when he saw it—a huge mushroom cloud with an orange belly, oozing up from the new row houses across from the high school. He threw his hand in front of his eyes. His pencil bounced off the desk and clattered onto the floor.

"Pitman?" Mr. Channing asked. "You all right, Pitman?"

The cloud had disappeared. Behind the row houses there was nothing but a blue December sky. Jeff shook his head at the algebra teacher and leaned down for his pencil. The algebra test was a blur of blue lines and smudges. He picked the pencil up, gathered his books and notebooks from under the seat, and stumbled to the front of the room.

"You sick, Pitman?"

"Yeah, I think so. Like I'm gonna throw up or something." He didn't bother to ask Channing to let him finish the test later. He just handed it over and walked out of the school, back to the apartment. His mother would be furious. No, not furious. Before the divorce she got furious; now she got hurt or hysterical. He preferred furious, but then nobody was asking him.

The mail had come. He picked up *Newsweek* to read while he drank his milk. There was a picture of a mushroom cloud on the cover. His skin prickled all over, and he dropped the magazine to the floor. Not the milk. He was lucky it wasn't the milk.

At least that was a real picture of an atomic blast, not a hallucination. Because during the next few days, he saw, or thought he saw, the orange-bellied cloud three more times—once in English class and twice in nightmares.

Then school was out for the holidays. Several days before Christmas, Jeff went downtown, determined to do his shopping, although he didn't even want to think about Christmas. It brought back too many memories —like candlelight in church, and caroling, and huge, sweet-smelling trees—and the time when he was about three when his father took him to see the department-store Santa Claus.

Just as Jeff had gotten to the head of the line, the bearded guy had looked him straight in the eye and boomed out, "Ho! Ho! Ho!" Jeff had screamed for his daddy, and he had come running and picked Jeff up. And his daddy hadn't been embarrassed or anything. In fact, he'd fussed at the Santa for laughing so loud and scaring little kids. Jeff still remembered how his father had carried him all the way home.

"That wasn't the real Santa Claus," he had told Jeff. "Just a make-believe. A fake. Didn't even know how to laugh." And they'd both giggled at how stupid the old guy had been. . . . It had been a long time since the two of them had giggled together.

Jeff was going up the escalator, half-listening to the rinky-dink carols being played on the department store loudspeaker—they were as fake as that old Santa's laugh had been—when he saw the mushroom cloud again, right inside the department store, against the wall above the men's sweaters.

"Watch out! What do you think you're doing?" But Jeff ignored the protests, pushing his way down the up escalator as fast as he could and out the front door of the store.

He was breathing hard and sweating despite the cold. "Peace on the earth . . ." God, what a laugh. He was almost crying.

He began walking out rapidly from the center of town. How long before it will all be gone? he wondered. Exploding in the sky or smothered in freezing darkness—either way it would all be gone. A stray dog watched him coming and waited until Jeff drew alongside, lifting its nose and staring with sad brown eyes into Jeff's face.

He knows, Jeff thought. Just a dumb mutt, and he knows.

There were ropes of red and silver strung between the light posts, and on each post a plastic candle in dirty yellow.

What man would destroy, he first makes rinky-dink. Jeff kicked a beer bottle someone had thrown down. It skimmied across the pavement and crashed against concrete steps.

"Hey, watch it!" The screech came from an old

woman who was sitting on the steps. "Ain't you got no respect?"

"I'm sorry." Jeff began to pick up the shattered brown glass.

"God's gonna get you, sonny." She jerked her head toward the building behind her. It was a large, graying stucco church. "God's gonna get you good."

"I really am sorry."

She must have been wearing four or five layers of clothes, and her head was wrapped in rags. He could even see the dingy lace of an ancient slip hanging out from under the tatters. Beside her on the steps were two large shopping bags. She reached into one of them and dug around, finally bringing out a large blue kerchief. She blew her nose noisily.

Then, suddenly, she began to cough—coughs that shook her whole body and seemed almost to shake the concrete step beneath her. Her face grew crimson, then almost blue, and she was choking, hardly able to breathe.

"Are you okay?" Jeff moved toward her, wondering what he should do. She shook him away.

Once more she reached into her bag and pulled out a bottle and a tablespoon that had lost most of its silverplate. Still coughing and gagging, she shakily poured some of the brown liquid into the spoon and jammed it into her mouth. It dribbled out the corners. She licked her lips and sent a long tongue down toward her whiskery chin.

"So? What are you staring at?"

"Nothing. I'm sorry." Jeff busied himself once more picking up the broken glass. He stood up, looking for a trash receptacle.

"Here," she said, holding out a sheet of newspaper.

"Thanks." He dropped the glass onto the paper, intending to throw it all away, but she drew back her hand and, folding the paper over the glass, put it into her shopping bag.

"Never know when it will come in handy," she said. "Ain't that right?"

"Sure," he said. "Sure."

"You think I'm crazy, don't you?"

"No, not at all."

"Liar."

For the first time in months, Jeff was beginning to enjoy himself. He had met a genuine original bag lady of the streets. "You're no crazier than me."

She cocked her head. "You don't look crazy—little stupid, maybe, not crazy."

"Oh, but you don't know. I—I see things." He had meant to joke, but in the middle, the familiar chill spurted through his body. Why had he said it?

"Yeah?" Her pale grayish eyes were glittering. "What do you see?" she asked.

He swallowed hard. Maybe if he told someone . . . "Clouds," he said, "mushroom clouds. Scares the devil out of me." He tried to smile, but his mouth stuck.

Something stirred behind the old eyes. "Like Japan? In the war?"

He nodded.

She sniffed, wiping her nose on a grubby rag. "Crazy not to be scared of that."

The chill passed. He liked the woman more every minute. "Mind if I sit down?"

"I don't. The reverend highness William P. Prisspot might." She pulled her shopping bags closer to make room for him.

"The reverend who?" he asked, wishing he'd thought to sit upwind of her.

"Aw, the preacher at this so-called church. He thinks I lower the property values or something, sitting on his fancy steps. God awmighty, at least I don't break beer bottles all over them."

"I said I was sorry."

"You don't want any supper, do you?"

"What? Oh, no, thanks," he said as she brought a white McDonald's sack from the shopping bag and took out what remained of a well-chewed hamburger.

"You'd be surprised what people throw away," she said, moving the hamburger around to where there were teeth to bite it.

"Mrs. Dodson!" The brown wooden door had opened behind them, and a man in a dark suit and blue tie was towering above them.

"Whoppedo," the old woman said through her burger. "It's neighborhood cleanup time."

The man came down the stairs and stood on the pavement in front of them, but he still seemed to be towering over them. "Mrs. Dodson, what are you doing here?"

Jeff was more surprised by the fact that the old woman had a name than by the fact that the minister knew it.

"I thought you were all settled into Friendship House."

"Oh, Preach, that place is worse than the slammer. I can't stay there. It's a bunch of eighty-year-old pickpockets and streetwalkers. What's an honest old lady like me gonna do in a dump like that?"

"In the first place, Mrs. Dodson, you're about as honest as Jesse James. And in the second place, you're sick and have no business sleeping on the street in this weather."

"Well, it's your fault. If you'd let me sleep on one of them nice red-cushioned benches in there . . ."

"Mrs. Dodson, you know I can't let you do that."

"It's not as if you was crowded to the doors. You hardly got half a house Sunday morning, and you sure as Christmas don't have anybody there at night."

"It's a church, Mrs. Dodson, not a motel. Besides, it's not really up to me."

"Next you'll be telling me God won't let you."

"I'm afraid God doesn't have much to say about it. It's the church board that makes policies about the use of the building, and *they* feel you'd be much more comfortable in Friendship House."

"Well, Friendship House don't happen to suit me. I'm very sorry." She jabbed Jeff with her elbow. "That's your line, ain't it, sonny?" She put her palm on her chest and lifted her head. "I'm sorry, Reverend, so sorry, so very sorry." The old lady was an actress. He loved her.

"Would you introduce me to your young friend,

Mrs. Dodson?" the minister asked, interrupting her performance.

"What? Oh, the kid." She considered Jeff. "Just some crazy delinquent took up with me. Don't worry. I'll trash *him* before nighttime. The board wouldn't want him on their fancy benches."

"Does he have a name?" the minister asked, smiling at Jeff.

"Even a dog's got a name," she grumped. "I just don't happen to want to tell you. You'd ship him off to Friendship House to rot."

"Oh, come on, now, Mrs. Dodson. We're only trying to help."

"Yeah, that's what the snake said to Eve."

Jeff caught the minister's eye and they both started laughing. Jeff couldn't help himself. The woman was priceless.

"You see why I let this woman drive me crazy, don't you?" the man said.

Jeff nodded. Mrs. Dodson humphed and went back to chewing at her used hamburger.

"Mrs. Dodson," the minister said, "tell you what. You go back to Friendship House just for tonight. It's going to be freezing. Just go back there this one night, and by tomorrow I'll find you another place."

"Not the slammer."

"No."

"Not the state hospital."

He raised three fingers in a salute. "Scout's honor," he said.

She pretended to consider it. "How about five dollars for a nice warm supper? This hamburger's about wore out."

"You remember what you did with the five dollars I gave you last week?"

"Cough syrup. I got this terrible cough." She coughed a bit to prove it.

The minister pulled a wallet from his pocket. He took out a five-dollar bill. The woman reached for it, but he handed it to Jeff instead. "Would you do me a favor and take her down to the café at the corner of Fifth and Main and see that she gets some solid food in her? Now don't go pouting, Mrs. Dodson. You know what would happen to this money if I gave it to you."

She wouldn't let Jeff help carry the shopping bags. She insisted on dragging them herself the five blocks to the café. At least once on every block she fell into a fit of coughing, bending over with her rag-wrapped head nearly to the pavement.

At last he pushed open the café door and waited as she hauled herself and her possessions the last few feet into the warmth. "Hey, Rosie," someone yelled. "I see they let you out."

"Shut up," she replied pleasantly. She was obviously at ease here. "I got money," she said to the waitress, a woman of about sixty years with the build of a linebacker, "and I'll have the special." She turned to Jeff anxiously. "You hungry?"

"No," he said.

She smiled happily. "Too bad." She settled back. "A tall draft for me, Gert. And how 'bout"—she smiled mischievously—"how 'bout a side order of mushrooms for the boy?"

He flushed and began to fiddle with the edge of the paper napkin. The old woman leaned toward him. "Now don't let a little teasing curl your upper plate, sonny."

"It's okay," he said, not looking up. "The whole thing's pretty stupid. I know that."

"Be stupid not to be scared," she said.

He looked up. She was smiling at him. "You really think so?"

"Sure. You never know what those Japs'll do."

He almost started to explain to her that the Japanese had nothing to do with his fears, but it seemed too complicated, so he just smiled back.

The food came. It was all the same color—a thick white gravy covered the meat loaf and mashed potatoes, and there were white beans on the side. But she ate with enthusiasm. "Wanna bite?"

"No, thanks. My mom's expecting me."

"That's sweet," she said. "You having a mother. I figured you for a stray."

"Not quite," he said.

When she had finished, wiping the plate clean with a piece of white bread and lifting her empty glass three times to try to squeeze out another drop, she gave a big sigh and sagged back against the booth.

It was well past dusk outside. His mother would be hysterical. "How are you going to get to Friendship House?" he asked.

She looked up sharply. "It's only a couple blocks from here. I can walk her. No rush."

He hesitated.

"You better run along home. I want to just sit here for a while before committing myself to that fruit basket."

"You'll be all right?"

"Sonny, I been all right for seventy-eight years, which is more than I can say for you."

He paid Gert at the cash register. "I hope you didn't leave my tip on the table. Rosie will steal it, sure," Gert said as she took his money.

He flushed. He'd forgotten the tip, so he handed her the change. "It's from the church," he said.

"Yeah," she said. "I figured. What a bum."

"She's not a bum." Why on earth was he defending her? Of course she was a bum. But he hated the waitress for saying it. He borrowed a pencil and took a napkin off the counter and wrote his phone number on it. He walked back to the booth. "Here," he said, pulling a quarter from his pocket. "This is my phone number. In case you need somebody."

"You are crazy, ain't you?"

"Yep," he said. They both smiled.

HIS MOTHER WAS only slightly hysterical. He pretended to be offended by her so that he wouldn't have to talk during supper. He didn't want to have to explain that he was late because he had been taking a bag lady out to dinner.

He went to bed, thinking more about that crazy old woman than the end of the world. But once asleep, the nightmares returned. There was the blinding flash of light. He raised his arm to shield his face and he saw his own bones through the flesh. An alarm began to ring. He sat up sweating. It was the telephone.

He jumped out of bed, ran to the kitchen, and snatched it up. He was still panting.

"Sonny?"

"Who is this?"

"It's Rosie. Who's this?"

"It's me, Rosie. You woke me up."

"That's what you get for sleeping."

His mother was calling from her bedroom, asking who was on the phone. He covered the mouthpiece. "Just this girl I know, Mom. It's okay." She grumbled about telephone calls at ungodly hours, but he knew she liked the idea that some girl was calling him. Hoo-haw, what a girl.

"You still there, sonny?"

He cupped his hand around the receiver and spoke as quietly as he could. "Where are you? Are you all right?"

She began to cough in answer, choking and gasping.

"Rosie? Where are you?"

"I'm in the church," she managed to say. "It's cold as Hades in here. I think they turned off the stinking heat." She began to cough again. "I don't feel so great," she gasped out at last.

"I'm coming," he said.

"Side door," she managed to say before another spasm of coughing.

When he got to the side door of the church, it was open. He slipped in. Except for the red glow from the exit lights, it was pitch dark. He fumbled instinctively for a switch, but realized in time that more light was sure to bring the police.

"Rosie," he called softly, feeling his way down the corridor. "Rosie, where are you?" He heard her coughing and followed the sound. He could make out the dim outline of the pulpit to his left and the pews stretching back to his right. The smell of greenery spiced the cold air. "Rosie?"

She was slumped over in a pew near the front. He felt her forehead the way his mother used to feel his when he was small.

"I don't feel so good," she said.

"I think you have a fever," he said. "Shouldn't you go to a hospital?"

"Who do you think I am, sonny, Mrs. Nelson B. Vanderbilt?"

"If you go, they gotta take you in."

"We already figured out you was crazy, right?"

He sat down beside her. Her old face glowed red from the exit light over the side entrance.

"You see things, don't you, sonny?"

"Yeah."

"Can you see if I'm gonna die tonight or not?"

The idea of her dying was like looking at his own bones through his arm. "You're not going to die, Rosie."

"I'm gonna die. Maybe not tonight. But sometime soon enough."

"Don't say that."

"You care, don't you?" She twisted around to try to look at him. "That's kinda sweet." She settled back. "I like that."

They sat there in the silent darkness, her shoulder against his. Hers was wrapped in so many layers of clothing that there didn't seem to be a human body underneath, but there was. He knew there was.

"I'm scared, you know. I ain't been all that good. I figger God's gonna get me something awful."

He opened his mouth to reassure her when, suddenly, he saw it. A plain wooden cross hung from the beams over the pulpit, and right behind the cross, swelling up from the shadows at the back wall, the form of the terrible mushroom cloud. He punched her shoulder. "There, Rosie, you see it?"

She jerked her eyes open. "What? See what, sonny?"

"The cloud—there, right behind the cross."

"God awmighty. We're a pair." Then she hunched her shoulders and squinted. "That ain't no cloud, sonny. That's one of them fancy glass windows. Look again. That's angel's wings. See, there in the window. It's an angel."

And it was an angel—an angel bending over talking to a woman.

"Fear not." He said it out loud.

"What, sonny?"

"That's what the angel said, 'Fear not.' "

"That's sweet," she said. "I like it." She stretched out away from him on the bench, shoving his jacket with her tennis shoes so that he stood up. She sighed. "Maybe God ain't out to get me after all. Sent me my own private angel. Might be a crazy angel, but he's sweet." She punched the air in Jeff's direction so that he would know she was joking.

Jeff took off his jacket and put it over her legs, but it was hardly enough. He went back into the hall and nosed about until he found the choir room, which had a closet full of robes. He grabbed a handful from the rack and took them back to the sanctuary. He began covering her with the robes, but she seemed so quiet. What if she had died on him, here in this cold church? What could he do? "Rosie," he called softly. Then louder, "Rosie!"

She didn't move. All he had done was go to the choir room, and now she was dead.

"Rosie," he called hoarsely. "Are you all right?" Oh, God, don't let her die.

The old woman opened one eye. "Fear not," she said. "Fear not, sonny. Just get my bags from the ladies' room and get on home before your mother calls the cops."

He brought her bags. "Are you going to be okay?"

She snuggled under the mound of choir robes. "Sleeping in heavenly peace, sonny." She cackled. "Didn't know I knew that line, did you now?"

He patted her and took one last look at the angel over the altar. If he'd known how to pray properly, Jeff would have thanked someone. "Take care of her," he said to the angel or God or Jesus—whoever watched out for old bag ladies and crazy kids.

It was black outside, and bitter cold without his jacket. Above the darkened streets, the sky sagged under a load of stars. But there was one star, far more brilliant than the rest, its light almost touching the shadows of the houses—like a flaming solitary dancer low in the eastern sky.

Maybe he was seeing things again. Rosie was right. He was crazy. But this time he was not afraid.

A slightly different version of this story was published in The Big Book for Peace, *eds. Ann Durell and Marilyn Sachs. Dutton Children's Books, 1990.*

Merit Badges

"Scouts," Mrs. Bushey was saying, "we are entirely too involved in ourselves." It was all I could do to keep from snickering out loud. I didn't dare look at Amy. We'd both collapse. Mrs. Bushey always said "scouts," not "girls" or "kids" like a normal grown-up, or "students" like a teacher.

How did the woman ever get to be a scout leader, anyhow? I wondered. Well, of course, Judy quit to have a baby. That's how. They were desperate for somebody—anybody—to take over. But where would you dig up someone like Bushey? All of us called her Bushey behind her back. It absolutely fit. She had a bad home permanent that frizzed all over her strange little round head and she never shaved her legs. She was a sight.

"What?" I hadn't been paying attention. Apparently, Bushey had been plowing ahead with some harebrained scheme (no pun intended).

"Are we agreed then, Scout Hensen?"

"Sure, okay." What in the world had I agreed to do? I'd have to ask Amy afterward.

"Then here are the names of the residents and a little bit about each. We won't be able to make special friends with every one. We just wouldn't have the time, what with our busy school and activity schedules, would we?" Why did Bushey always say "we"? Didn't the woman know any other pronouns? *Residents?* I suddenly heard the word. What was Bushey talking about? What residents?

"There," said Bushey happily, "we have made a start in caring. We scouts must endeavor to be caring persons, mustn't we?"

The ten of us somehow got through Bushey's closing ceremony of the scout pledge and a song about friendship that must have been written about the time of the *Mayflower*.

We stumbled out of the dark church basement into

the late afternoon sunshine. But not before every other member of the troop was looking at me, their smirks exploding into shrieks. "Ah-ha, Kate, Bushwhacked, Bushwhacked." Amy had made up that term for anyone in the troop who let Bushey sucker her into something.

"What do you mean? I didn't get Bushwhacked. I wanted to."

"You're lying." Amy stared at me.

Now I was caught. I couldn't admit that I had no idea what I'd promised to do.

"Kate! You know perfectly well what happened when Judy took us there last Christmas."

"Christmas?" Here was a clue.

"The caroling. The 'disaster of the decade!' " That's what Judy had called our attempt to cheer up the residents at Logan Manor. My skin began to creep. Had I promised to do something at the manor? "That was just one crazy old woman," I said nervously.

"Sto—op!" Amy yelled. "Stop the noise!" imitating the old woman who had raced out of her room while we were singing "Silent Night." We'd been scared silly at the time, but now it was one of our group jokes. Whenever we wanted to make each other giggle, somebody would began imitating the old lady who had driven us out of the nursing home where we had gone to carol last Christmas.

All the others joined in. "Sto—op! Stop the noise!"

"So?" I pretended not to care. "She's not the only person there. I don't have to try to cheer *her* up. I can choose someone else."

"Aren't we a *good* scout?" Laura pinched her mouth in a perfect imitation of Bushey. "Shut up, Laura," I muttered. I could just see Bushey's frizzed head coming up the steps out of the basement.

It was bedtime before I looked at the list that Bushey had given me. It was typed, but obviously by someone who could barely do so. There were twenty-six names on the list. All women. All old. There were stars beside about ten of the names. At the bottom it said: "*These residents have no one who comes to visit on a regular basis." There were four names that had double stars. "**These residents have no visitors."

Suddenly I felt freezing cold. I put on my bathrobe and went downstairs. My mother was still in the kitchen packing lunches for the next day. "Mom?"

"Katie. I thought you were already in bed."

"I'm just going."

She looked at me for a minute. "Is something the matter?"

"No." I felt silly and about four years old. "I guess—I guess I just wanted to come down and make sure you were here," I said.

She smiled. "Where else would I be, Pumpkin?" It was a baby name she hardly ever used anymore.

I kissed her cheek. "I love you, Mom."

"I love you, too. Now off to bed with you."

IT WAS A couple of days before I looked at the list again. By this time I'd decided several things. One, I would not choose anyone who *never* had visitors. That was likely to get me the stop-the-noise crazy one in that bunch. If I was going to do this—and none of my friends believed for a minute that I had the nerve—I would have to choose someone who wouldn't run me off or scare me to death.

On the other hand, it didn't seem quite fair to choose someone who already had regular visitors. That left the ten one-starred residents. The ones on this list with scary descriptions like "probable Alzheimer's" or "unable to speak" or "deaf" I crossed off. We were a scout, not a doctor or a psychologist, right? We were not going to bite off more than we could chew and give our friends the satisfaction of seeing us fail.

This got the list down to three residents. I chose Mildred Hull (husband deceased, no children, likes to play cards) because if you couldn't think of anything to say, you could always play cards. And besides, if the woman could play cards, she couldn't be totally off her rocker.

Monday afternoon was scout meeting. I was determined to make my first visit before then, but Sunday came and I still hadn't gone. I was tempted to ask Mom to go with me. But she and Dad had promised to do something at church. I dragged out my scout uniform, which had been in the closet since the "disaster of the decade." The sleeves cut me under the arms, and I looked really doofy. But I told myself it was like wearing a costume for Halloween. You could be someone else dressed up. I guess I needed the protection.

At the desk near the front door was a very skinny woman with an enormous head of hair that made her look lopsided. I bit the inside of my cheek to keep from giggling.

"Yes, honey?" the woman said. She didn't look like the kind of woman that would call you honey, but never mind. I cleared my throat. "I'm here to see Mrs. Hull," I said.

"Who?"

"Mrs. Mildred Hull." From barely a croak I went to a boom, and the woman ducked her head as if to say, "They're deaf, not me."

But all she said was: "Is Mildred expecting you?"

"Oh." I should have called. It was a little late to think of that now. "I don't think so. I'm Kathryn Hensen—I'm—from the Girl Scouts."

"Where is your leader?" That's what the aliens always want to know. I shrugged. Let her think my leader forgot or something.

She considered me. "Well," she said finally, "why don't you wait here while I go and see what Mildred's up to. A lot of our little people like to take a nap in the afternoon." Her voice dropped to a whisper as though she was letting me in on a big secret.

There was nothing to do but stand there by the desk while old women shuffled past, staring me up and down as if I was an endangered species in the zoo. The label of my uniform scratched the back of my neck, and I could feel the seams cutting the flesh under my arms. I should have worn something comfortable. But it was too late now.

Finally, the receptionist came trotting back. "This is Mildred," she said.

I was buffaloed. The receptionist was standing there all alone. For a minute I thought one of her "little people" was invisible, and then I realized that, clumping slowly up the long corridor behind a walker, was an old, old woman who must be Mildred Hull (husband deceased, no children).

I didn't know whether to run down the hall and stop the poor old thing from making the torturous trip all the way to the front desk or just to stand there and wait, trying not to stare.

"Mildred says she doesn't know you," said the receptionist as though to fill the time. "But some of our little people get confused."

Our little people? "No," I said. "No, she wouldn't have any way of knowing me."

"But wasn't your group here at Christmas, or was that some other—?"

"Uh, Mrs. Hull?" I double-stepped it down the hall toward the bent figure.

The white head twisted up, the arms leaning heavily on the metal frame. "Last time I checked," she said. "And you?"

"We—I'm Kate Hensen. I'm a Girl Scout." What were you supposed to say?

"Oh, I get it. I couldn't imagine why any young

girl I never heard of was coming to see me. I'm a merit badge."

"No. Really."

"Let me be a merit badge, please. I don't think I'm up to being a good deed for the day."

I guess I just stood there with my mouth open.

"If it's any comfort, our uniforms were worse. Lots worse." I tried to smile. "Well, if I can't get you a merit badge, what can I do for you?" she asked.

"Maybe we could sit down somewhere?"

"Sure. No stamina, you kids today. No stamina."

She clumped her way to the little sitting area near the front door. I followed her, my hands out ready to catch the woman if she stumbled. I hovered around while she heaved herself into a straight chair and then nodded at me to take the overstuffed one next to it.

"Tell me about yourself," the old woman said, after she had caught her breath from the trip down the hall. "I haven't seen a live child close-up for ages. What are you like?"

"Like? Me?"

"Yeah. What would you be doing for example if you hadn't been shamed into coming to visit some poor little old lady today?"

"I— What?"

"Oh, come on now Kathryn or Kitty or—?"

"Kate. Everyone calls me Kate."

"Is that what you want to be called?"

"Well, yeah, I guess so."

"I like to call people what they want to be called."
She lowered her voice and leaned toward me. "Stick,
there," she whispered, jerking her head toward the
receptionist, "calls me Mildred. I hate it."

"Stick?"

"Yeah, shhhh. We call her that because she looks
like those stick figures little kids draw. You know."

I giggled out loud. I couldn't help myself.

"All these young aides here call me Mildred,
too. I hate it. No one in my life ever called me
Mildred."

"What do you want to be called?"

"My friends used to call me Millie." She leaned
toward me again. "Promise you won't tell?"

I nodded, even though I had no idea what I was
promising.

"My older brother used to call me Mildew."

"Mildew?" I looked at the woman, trying to see a
little girl with a brother who called her Mildew. It was
hard to imagine.

"For years, I burst into tears every time he said it," she said. "Silly, huh?"

"My brother used to call me Spook," I said.

"Spook?"

"My birthday is on Halloween. I hated that nick-name. My mom calls me Pumpkin sometimes, and I don't mind at all."

"It's the way she says it, right?" She was quiet for a minute. "Ralph was my brother's friend. I was sev-enteen when I met him, and let me tell you the minute I saw that man I knew I wanted to marry him. When my brother introduced me as his sister, 'Mildew,' I was ready to kill him." She shook her head. "You know what Ralph called me till the day he died? Dewy." She gave her head a little shake. "Dewy. I thought it was the most beautiful name a girl could ever have."

I stared at her face hidden by thick, smudged glasses, trying hard to see that teenage girl so crazy with love. Then I realized Mrs. Hull was staring back and I said quickly, "Would you like to play some cards?"

"Cards? Why would I want to play cards? I hate cards."

"The, uh—" How could you tell a person they were on a list (husband deceased, no children)? "They—uh—told me you liked to play cards."

"I play cards. Sure. With people who can't make conversation. Why should I play with you?" She cocked her head. "I guess we scare kids, don't we, with our white heads and false teeth and all our handicaps and infirmities. Yeah, I guess that's it. We're like monsters, aren't we, to healthy children like you."

"No," I said, "really." But I felt a tingle as I said it.

"I thought we'd never see anyone under the age of fifty in here again after last Christmas."

"Last Christmas?"

"A bunch of kids—Girl Scouts, too. I remember the uniforms. They came in here all brave and shiny to give the poor old coots some holiday cheer—" She started to giggle. "You're not going to believe this—"

Try me.

"My roommate. She's a harmless old soul, but they woke her out of a sound sleep. And right in the middle of these little girls sweetly chirping away, she comes roaring out of the room screaming her head off. Those little green girls ran like Frankenstein himself was upon them." She started to laugh. "I'm sorry," she said, "it does seem mean to laugh, but it was the funniest sight we've had around here since Stick got her new hairdo. We'll never forget that night." She looked at me sharply. "You think we're cruel? Getting so much fun at the expense of those poor scared children?"

I shook my head. "Someday they will probably look back on it and laugh," I said.

"We take our fun where we can get it around here," she said, almost as if apologizing. "I really don't approve of making fun of people"—she jerked her head toward the receptionist—"with perhaps the one major exception. I used to say to my daughter, June, I'd say—"

Daughter?

"What's the matter? Oh. If I have a daughter, why am I here? Or why doesn't she come to see me? Is that it?"

"Well, they said—"

"She's dead."

What were you supposed to say to something like that? I opened my mouth, but there were no words.

"It was a long time ago. But it's hard, you know. No, of course you don't know. You're what? Ten? Eleven?"

"Almost twelve."

"I hope you never know. I thought when Ralph died I would never get over it, but losing your child —having your beautiful child die— Why should I be the one to live on and on?" she asked angrily. "What is my life worth? It isn't right," she said more quietly. "It's just not right." She fumbled around in the sleeve of the old housedress she was wearing. "Excuse me," she said. "This is embarrassing, but when I left my room, I didn't seem to bring a tissue."

I rooted in my pocket and pulled out a very wrinkled Kleenex. Mrs. Hull took off the thick glasses and wiped her eyes. "Thank you," she said. "You can mention that for the merit badge. Always be prepared. Or something like that. Don't tell them it was used. They may take off points."

"WE DON'T SUPPOSE we have anything to report about our project at Logan Manor?" Bushey looked wistful, like a kid asking Santa for a toy that she knew she wasn't going to get.

"I went Sunday afternoon," I said. The rest of the troop turned in their chairs to stare, but Bushey was smiling. She had a nice smile. She ought to smile more often.

"Yeah, I went through the list and picked a person they said didn't have any regular visitors. I didn't want to be running competition to somebody's darling grandchild."

"Did you get—you know who?" Laura whispered loudly.

"Who?" asked Bushey.

"This woman we met when we were caroling last year. No," I said to the others, "I was pretty careful about that." They laughed nervously.

"And?"

"Her name was Mrs. Hull and she said she didn't want to be my merit badge"—I ignored the noises the others were making—"but that she'd rather be a merit badge than a good deed."

"Which was she?" Amy asked.

"Neither. I liked her. I think she likes me, too. I'm going back to see her next week."

But Tuesday night Bushey called. The receptionist had made a mistake. Unaccompanied minors were not allowed to visit residents. "We could go with you," Bushey said.

"No!" As soon as I yelled it, I was sorry. "It's not you, Mrs. Bushey, it's the principle of the thing. I'm not going to misbehave. And I'm not going to give her some disease. I just want to talk with her. It wouldn't be the same with another person listening over our shoulders."

"If you're not comfortable with us, your mother might—"

"No, Mrs. Bushey, it's not you, really. I don't want my mother, either. I don't want to have to be baby-sat when I'm visiting with a friend."

"We understand," Bushey said, "and we think you're absolutely right. We will call the owner."

"Thanks, Bushey," I said, not even realizing that I'd forgotten the "Mrs.," "but I think Mrs. Hull and I can handle this."

"May we say how proud we are, Scout Hensen?"

"Sure," I said.

I called Logan Manor immediately, but the night person told me that it was too late for calls. "It's only eight," I said.

"Our little people need their rest." Apparently the night person was a Stick clone.

The next afternoon, they let me talk to Mrs. Hull who was, as I was sure she would be, outraged.

"You come over here and we'll give that Mervin Wertz a piece of your mind. At my age, I don't have any to spare. And don't wear your uniform. Wear something that fits and makes you look like your parents could buy this place out and have money left over to burn."

When I arrived, dressed in the suit that my grandmother had sent me for Easter, Stick was on duty. I even wore my only pair of panty hose. I had started to sneak some of Mom's makeup, but I was afraid she'd make a fuss.

"Oh yes, Kathy, isn't it?" Stick was rigid (pun intended).

"Kate Hensen. I think Mrs. Hull made an appointment for the two of us to speak to Mr. Wertz."

"Mildred and Gracie are already in his office," she said.

I opened the door. A man, a shriveled little man, was seated behind an enormous desk. Standing in front of him was Mrs. Hull, leaning on her walker with one hand and pounding on it with the other. In a chair on the opposite side of the room sat the person who Stick called Gracie, better known to me as "Stop-the-Noise." My blood froze, but I went into the room.

Mrs. Hull was saying something that ended with ". . . the Constitution of the United States of America."

Mr. Wertz was getting very small and very pale. Everyone turned to look at me. I was glad I'd dressed so carefully.

"Is this the child?" Mr. Wertz asked.

"She has a name!" Mrs. Hull shouted. "She has a name. She is a person!"

"Kate Hensen," I said. "How do you do, Mr. Wertz?" I walked over and offered him my hand. I was so polite and mature my grandmother would have fainted with joy.

Mr. Wertz ignored my hand. "It's very sweet of you little girls to want to cheer up our residents" (at least he didn't say "little people"), "but this is a medical and nursing facility, not a day care center." He smiled. I guess he thought it was a little joke. "We have some residents"—he gave Gracie a nervous glance—"who may be upset by unsupervised young visitors. And well, sometimes children are upset by elderly residents who, well, how shall I put it—?"

"Shut up!" Stop-the-Noise had jumped to her feet.

"As you see—"

"Shut up, I said!"

Mr. Wertz blinked rapidly. "Well, I don't really feel that we need to discuss this further. Our Gracie—"

"I'm not your Gracie!"

Mr. Wertz must have rung a bell or something because a young woman in a white uniform was there almost immediately. She took Gracie, or whatever Mrs. Hull's roommate was really named, by the arm and led her out of the room, shutting the door behind them. I could hear the old woman shouting down the hall as she went.

"You see, my dear, little children"—again my grandmother would have been proud that I didn't correct him—"sometimes, without even meaning to, can have an upsetting effect."

"Mr. Wertz, excuse me, but I think she was upset by you, not by me."

"She's right," Mrs. Hull said. "Mrs. Ticknor hates being called Gracie."

"We always call our people by their first names," Mr. Wertz said.

"I know," said Mrs. Hull, "and some of us always hate it."

I left that one alone. "Mr. Wertz," I said, "Mrs. Hull and I are friends—not close friends, I admit. We haven't had time for that. But we'd like to get to know each other better. We can't do that with chaperons. Frankly, we find the idea insulting. We are both perfectly intelligent people. I promise you that if you will allow me to come and visit Mrs. Hull, you will not regret it." I tried to put into my voice a hint that my family had untold millions, some of which would surely be donated to his nursing home if he agreed, but I can't be sure all that came through.

"And if it's any comfort to you, Mr. Wertz," said Mrs. Hull, "I will try to behave just as beautifully as my friend here."

"Whew," she said as we escaped after our triumph to a private corner of the lounge. "That was a near thing."

"Yeah," I said. "What's-her-name, Gracie, I mean—"

"Mrs. Ticknor to you," Mrs. Hull said. "Yeah, great, wasn't she?"

"What?"

"Yeah, right on cue. We couldn't have done it without her. Remind me to pick up a Hershey bar for her. Kind of our merit badge system. You know how it goes."

"I'm learning," I said.

BUSHEY AND I dragged the whole troop over to Logan Manor at Christmastime. Not to carol. Mrs. Hull vetoed that. We had a sing with the residents. Bushey, to my amazement, plays a mean piano, and Stick, when she unbends a bit, has a nice alto voice. Stick and I passed out songbooks, and the Girl Scouts scattered among the crowd. Gracie, I mean Mrs. Ticknor, mostly listened quietly, but when we got to "Joy to the World," I could hear her off-key "repeat the sounding joy" over and over long after the rest of us had gone on to the third verse. I smiled at Mrs. Hull, who smiled at me, and then Stick, who smiled at both of us. We all smiled at Bushey, who had a smile as wide as the stripes on the flag. We were all joyful. I think it was the first time I really understood the meaning of the word.

The Handmaid
of the Lord

PEOPLE THINK WHEN your father is the minister that you get special favors, like you were God's pet or something. Rachel, for one, knew absolutely, positively that it was not true. God didn't love her better than Jason McMillan, who was getting an entire set of Mighty Morphin Power Rangers for Christmas. God didn't love her better than that Carrie Wilson, who was getting a new Barbie dollhouse with two new dolls, outfits included. Not that Rachel really wanted a Barbie dollhouse, or Power Rangers either, for that matter, but it was the principle of the thing. Carrie and Jason were getting what they asked Santa Claus for. When Rachel asked Santa for a horse, John and Beth just rolled their eyes. John and Beth were her older brother and sister. Beth was eleven and John, thirteen, and they thought they knew everything.

"But where would we keep a horse, Rachel?" her mother had asked. She was changing baby David's diapers and not paying Rachel much attention. "We live in the church manse. You know how small our yard is."

"Rachel," her father had said in his most patient voice, "what is Christmas really about? If all you think about is Santa Claus, you're going to miss the main event." Rachel's heart sank. When your father told you to think what Christmas was *really* about, she knew what that meant. It meant no horse. Not even a pony. Ministers' kids never got really good presents at Christmas. She should know that by now. It didn't count if you were naughty or nice. Gregory Austin had pulled the alarm last Sunday and made the fire trucks come in the middle of church service, but he was getting his own personal computer. His daddy had said so. Her daddy told everybody they were supposed to be God's servants. Like Jesus was. He didn't even mention presents.

So—no good presents. Rachel had given up on that. But a big role in the primary classes' Christmas play—that shouldn't be too much to ask for. She was by far the best actress in the second grade. *Plus* she went to Sunday school every single week, even when she had the sniffles, or it snowed so hard that she and John and Beth were the only kids there.

"Don't you think a kid who comes every single Sunday no matter if it's a blizzard should get a good part in the primary classes' play?" she asked.

"We live next door to the church, stupid," John had said. "You don't get brownie points for walking across your side yard."

"You're the minister's daughter, Rachel," Beth had said. "It would look bad if you grabbed a big part."

"You got to be Angel Gabriel in both the second *and* third grade," Rachel reminded her.

"That was different," Beth said. "I was the only one in either class who could remember all the lines. The head angel has a lot to say. Besides I speak out. Everyone in the back row heard me perfectly."

"I can speak out," Rachel said, but no one paid any attention.

When she was five, she had been part of the heavenly host. It was a terrible part. The angel costumes were made of a stiff gauzy stuff that itched something awful. Afterward Mrs. MacLaughlin, who ran the pageant, yelled at her right in front of everybody.

"Rachel Thompson! Angels are spiritual beings! They do not scratch themselves while they sing! You had the congregation laughing at the heavenly host. I was mortified."

Last year Mrs. MacLaughlin had taken a rest from directing, and Ms. Westford had run the pageant. Ms. Westford believed in equal opportunity, so for the first time in the history of First Presbyterian Church, girls had been shepherds and wise men. That was okay with the girls, but the boys were mad. They didn't like the itchy angel costumes at all. And a *lot* of the fathers complained.

But Rachel had been a much better shepherd than those stupid boys. She didn't care what anyone had said afterward. She knew what the Bible meant when it said the shepherds were "sore afraid." When Mr. Nelson shined the spotlight at them to show that the angel of the Lord was about to come upon them, Rachel had shown everyone in the church what it meant to be "sore afraid."

"Help! Help!" she'd cried loud enough to be heard by the people in the very back row. "Don't let it get me!"

The congregation laughed. So did Gabriel and all the shepherds and the entire heavenly host. Mary laughed so hard she started choking, and Joseph had to whack her on the back.

Her father said later that it had been "a brand-new insight on the Christmas story," and her mother said, "Never mind, dear, they weren't laughing at you." But she knew better. No one in the whole church understood what the story was really about. When the Bible said "sore afraid," you were supposed to be scared. When that big light hit her face, Rachel had been trembly all over. She knew in her heart that she was the only kid in the pageant who felt that way. Not even the second- and third-graders who got all the big parts did them right. If you couldn't have a scratching angel, you sure shouldn't have a Joseph yawning so wide you could drive a tractor trailer straight down to his tonsils.

It had been a hard year. Her mother had been tired and pregnant for most of it, and then when David finally was born she'd gotten tired and busy. Beth thought David was the "cutest thing in the world."

"Was I cute when I was little?" Rachel asked her.

"I can't remember," Beth said. "I know you cried

a lot. And your face got really red." And she went back to goo-gooing at the baby.

John wasn't as silly, but he was always bragging about how great it was to have a little brother *finally*.

"What's the matter with little sisters?" Rachel asked. John just rolled his eyes.

Now at the end of the worst year of her entire life, Christmas wasn't going to be any better. Even the carols were against her. All those songs about the City of David. "Couldn't we make up a Christmas song about the City of Rachel?" she asked her mother. But her mother just smiled and kept on singing about David.

"Hey," John said one night, "I just realized. We're all in the Christmas story—David, Elizabeth, John—"

"What about me?" Rachel said.

"Oh, you're in it," John said.

"I am?"

"Yeah. I can't remember the verse, but there's something off the side of the story about somebody named Rachel weeping and wailing."

"It's because King Herod killed all her children," Beth said.

It wasn't fair. Everyone else had a nice place in the story—everyone but Rachel. It made her more determined than ever to have a good part in the play, one in which she would not scratch or yell or wail. Mary. She would be Mary. She was old enough this year. She was the best actress in the second grade. Surely, even if she was the minister's daughter, Mrs. MacLaughlin would pick her. She'd be so good in class that Mrs. MacLaughlin would just see that nobody deserved to be Mary more than Rachel did.

Besides, her little brother had already been chosen to be Baby Jesus. She ought to be Mary. Jesus shouldn't have a stranger be his mother. It might scare him.

"Now," said Mrs. MacLaughlin at the first practice. "It's a good thing we have a lot of kindergarten to third-graders in this church because we have a lot of parts in this play."

"Mrs. MacLaughlin?" Rachel said.

"What is it, Rachel?" Mrs. MacLaughlin's voice sounded a tiny bit impatient, so Rachel talked fast.

"I know I'm the minister's kid and that when I was little, sometimes—"

"Yes, Rachel—"

"Well, I've studied the part really hard, and since my brother is the Baby Jesus, I thought, well, it would probably mean a lot to *him* if—well, if his big sister could be Mary."

"But we don't have sixth-graders in the play, Rachel. Elizabeth's too old."

"I don't mean Elizabeth, Mrs. MacLaughlin. I mean, well, what's the matter with me?"

There was a burst of laughter in the room. Everyone was laughing at her! Rachel's face went scarlet. "Shut up!" she yelled. "I'm serious. I know the story better than anybody here, and it's my brother!" Everyone laughed harder. Even the little ones who were going to be itchy angels were giggling.

"Rachel—dear—" said Mrs. MacLaughlin after she finally got control of the group. "Of course you know the Christmas story—after all, your father is our minister—but—but Mary is a very difficult role."

"I could do it," Rachel muttered, but she knew it was no use. People weren't supposed to laugh at Mary. And everybody laughed at her—when they paid her any attention at all.

"Carrie," Mrs. MacLaughlin was saying. "How would you like to be our Mary this year?"

Carrie Wilson? She had blue eyes and blond curls all the way down her back and didn't look at all like Mary. And that fake smile. It made Rachel sick to her stomach. Carrie Wilson's Mary would look like a plastic wimp. Mary was the handmaid of the

Lord, for heaven's sake, not some department-store dummy.

Rachel could hardly listen as Mrs. MacLaughlin went down the list telling everyone what they were supposed to be. She knew now she wouldn't even get a speaking part. Mrs. MacLaughlin didn't like her. Nobody liked her. Not even God. Finally, Mrs. MacLaughlin stopped.

Rachel looked up. She hadn't heard her name. She didn't want to say anything because maybe her name had been called when she wasn't listening and then Mrs. MacLaughlin would have something else to fuss about. But she couldn't stand it. She raised her hand.

"Yes, Rachel?"

"About my part—"

"Yes, Rachel. This year you have a *very* important part."

"I do?"

"Yes. You will be our understudy."

"Our what?"

"Since you know the story *so* well, you will be prepared to *substitute* in case any of our actors become ill or unable to perform."

"Substitute? You mean I don't have a part of my own?"

"You have *all* the parts—in case— Why suppose, for example, Gabriel should lose her voice? You would step in and be our Gabriel."

Jennifer Rouse, the third-grader who had been chosen to be Gabriel, gave Rachel a dirty look. She had no intention of losing her voice. "Or if"—here Mrs. MacLaughlin smiled sadly at Carrie Wilson—"our Mary were to suddenly have to visit her grandmother in Ohio, you would have to step in and be our Mary."

"My grandmother's coming *here* for Christmas, Mrs. MacLaughlin," Carrie said sweetly. Rachel wasn't stupid. She knew what Mrs. MacLaughlin was doing. She wasn't keeping Rachel from having a big part. She was making sure that Rachel wouldn't have any part at all.

SHE TOLD HER MOTHER that she was never going back to Sunday school again in her whole entire life. "Nonsense, dear," her mother said. And, of course, she went back. Ministers' children have to go to Sunday school. It's the law or something.

And then, a miracle happened. One week before Christmas, Carrie Wilson, who wore the world's prissiest little blue leather boots, slipped on the ice in the mall parking lot and broke both her arms. *Both* her arms. Rachel was overcome with exceeding great joy. God did love her. He did! One arm might count as an accident, but two arms were a miracle. God meant business. No matter how determined Mrs. Mac-Laughlin was to keep her out of the play, God was going to make sure not only that she got in but that she got the most important part in the whole shebang. She was going to be Mary, the handmaid of the Lord.

Of course, she didn't tell anybody how joyful she was. She was too smart for that. When Mrs. Mac-Laughlin called her on the phone, Rachel practically cried at the news that she would have to pinch-hit for our poor little Carrie. "I'll do my best, Mrs. Mac-Laughlin," she said quietly and humbly, just like the real Mary would have.

She went early to the dress rehearsal so Mrs. MacLaughlin could try the costume on her. It fit perfectly. Well, it would have fit practically anybody. Those robe things weren't exactly any size, but Rachel took it as a good sign when Mrs. MacLaughlin sighed and admitted that, yes, it did fit.

"Don't you worry, Mrs. MacLaughlin," Rachel said. "I'm the understudy. I know the part perfectly." Which was a little silly since Mary didn't say a word, just looked lovingly into the manger while everyone else sang and carried on. But she wanted Mrs. MacLaughlin to know she wasn't going to do anything to make anybody laugh this year. She would be such a good Mary that Mrs. MacLaughlin would be practically down on her knees begging her to take the part again next year. They'd probably have to extend the play past third grade so that they could keep Rachel in the role of Mary until she was grown up and through college and had babies of her own.

"We have to eat early," she told her mother on Christmas Eve. "Mrs. MacLaughlin wants the cast there an hour before the service."

"Thank goodness," said John. "I don't think I could stand another hour of loud glorias sung off-key."

But Rachel didn't care. She was so happy, the glorias just burst from her. Besides, she had to get them all out before seven o'clock. She couldn't let a stray gloria pass her lips when she was behind that manger. God might understand, but Mrs. MacLaughlin sure wouldn't.

She was all dressed in the sky-blue robe, sitting quietly, looking down into the empty manger. Mrs. MacLaughlin, hoarse from yelling at the heavenly hosts, was giving last-minute directions to the wise men, when suddenly the back door of the sanctuary opened.

"Why, Mrs. Wilson. Carrie——" Mrs. MacLaughlin said.

Rachel jerked up in alarm. It *was* Carrie, standing in the darkened sanctuary, her fake-fur-trimmed coat hanging off her shoulders, both arms bound to the front of her body.

"She insisted," Mrs. Wilson was saying. "She said, 'The show must go on.' I talked to Dr. Franklin, and he said it would be the best thing in the world for her. She was so distressed about letting everyone down that it was having a negative effect on the healing process——"

Two mothers yanked the beautiful blue robe off Rachel and draped it over Carrie's head. "See. It was meant to be," Mrs. Wilson said. "It totally hides the casts."

Rachel slunk off the platform and slumped down in the first pew. No one noticed. All the adults were oohing and ahing about how brave Carrie was to come and save the play.

"Oh, yes, she's in terrible pain," her mother was saying. "But she couldn't bear to disappoint you all."

No one cared that Rachel was disappointed. Not even God. Of course, God had known all along that

Carrie would show up at the last minute and steal back the part. God knew everything, and he had let Rachel sing and rejoice and think for a few days that he was on her side, that he had chosen her, like Mary, to be his handmaid. But it was just a big joke. A big, mean joke. She kicked the red carpet at her feet.

"Off stage, off stage, everyone. Time to line up in your places."

Where did you go when there wasn't any place for you? She looked around. People were beginning to arrive for the service. She slipped farther down in the pew. She didn't want her family to see her. They'd find out soon enough that God had fired her.

She saw her mother carry David up the far aisle. The baby was sucking happily on his pacifier. He would be a good Jesus. Everyone would say so. Mrs. MacLaughlin was waiting at the door to the hall. She took David and said something to Mom, who cocked her head in a doubtful manner. Was she telling Mom that Rachel wasn't going to be Mary after all? If she did, maybe Mom would come over and take her on her lap and tell her she was sorry. No, Mom didn't even look her way.

The play went well. None of the angels cried or scratched. Gabriel knew all her lines and said them loud enough to be heard almost to the back row. The wise men remembered to carry in their gifts and nobody's crown rolled off. Joseph did not yawn, and Mary gazed sweetly into the manger. It was all perfect. Perfect without her. Rachel felt like weeping and wailing like the Rachel in the Bible.

And then, suddenly, a miracle occurred. Baby Jesus began to cry. Not just cry, *scream*. Yell his little lungs out. Carrie Wilson forgot about being Mary. She turned absolutely white, and her eyes went huge, like she was about to panic. She would have probably got up and run, but with her arms bound under her robe she couldn't move. She looked at Joseph. "Do something!" she whispered. Joseph's face went bright red, but he didn't move a muscle.

It was all up to Rachel. She jumped from her pew and dashed up the chancel steps. She was still panting when she got to the manger. Rachel poked around under the baby until she located the pacifier and jammed it into David's open mouth. He clamped down on it at once. The big church went silent except for his noisy sucking. Rachel smiled down at him. He was a lovely Jesus.

"Who do you think you are?" Carrie Wilson hissed through her teeth. But the whisper was almost loud enough to be heard in the back row. Rachel could hear a snicker from somewhere out in the darkened sanctuary.

"Behold." Rachel straightened up and stared sternly in the direction of the offender. There was no doubt that the people in the last pew could hear her. "I am the handmaid of the Lord! And I say unto you, glory to God in the highest and on earth peace and goodwill to men, women, and children."

Nobody laughed. They didn't dare.

No Room
in the Inn

IN THE WINTER, our house looks like a Christmas card. It's an old Vermont farmhouse nestled into the woods, with a view of the snow-covered Green Mountains. The attached barn is now a garage, and my parents run a bed-and-breakfast in the house. My dad works full-time at a computer outfit, so, being both the only man and the only kid at home, I spend a lot of time splitting wood, making fires in the huge kitchen woodstove, cleaning rooms, changing sheets, washing dishes—you name it.

When I saw my parents off at Burlington Airport last week, I tried to look a little sad—as a Christmas present to my mother, who was feeling terrible about leaving me alone for the holidays. Can you imagine? An eighteen-year-old boy alone in a country inn with no guests to cater to, no wood to split, no beds to make—nothing to do for ten glorious days but eat, sleep, and ski. And a new Pontiac Grand Prix sitting in the other half of the garage whispering, "Use me! Use me! Use me!"

I had taken my folks to the airport in the 4 x 4. A good thing, too, because by the time I headed home, the snow was coming down hard. Great for the slopes, I thought, and switched on the radio, which was playing a sappy old-time number, "Let it Snow, Let it Snow, Let it Snow." I was feeling so good I listened to "White Christmas" and a jazzed-up version of "Away in a Manger" before I reached over to switch to my usual station. Ha! Ten days with no one complaining because I had switched the dial on the car radio.

I tried to figure out why I was feeling so great. Sure, I'd miss not having Christmas with the family. My sister's kids are terrific and they think their uncle Ben is God's gift to the world. But you have to understand. I never get time to myself these days. If I'm not working at school, I'm slaving away at the inn. It's really only a bed-and-breakfast, but my mother likes to call it The Inn. I'd have it all to myself, including the 4 x 4, which I have to share with my dad, and ta-da my mother's Pontiac, which for ten days was mine, all mine.

The euphoria had left me by the time I'd spent an hour and forty-five minutes driving what should have taken just over an hour. I was tired and hungry and feeling—could you believe it?—just a little bit sorry for myself in the blackness of a late winter afternoon when I turned off the interstate and headed for the village. I decided to stop at Gracie's, the only restaurant around for meat loaf and cheer. Gracie is famous for both.

The woodstove was crackling warm, and the smell of meat loaf and homemade bread filled the place. There were a couple of farmers, Ewell Biggs and Ames Whitehead, sitting at the counter drinking coffee when I got there. They nodded at me as I sat down. I nodded back, waiting for Gracie's usual "Hello, stranger!" But Gracie just stared at me sadly. "It's meat loaf tonight," she said, as though that would be the last thing anyone would want.

"That's fine," I said, and then, "is something the matter, Gracie?"

"Gracie's all worried about them Russians," Ewell explained to me between slurps of coffee.

"They're Armenians," Gracie said to him, and then to me, "I was just watching the news. Five hundred thousand with no place to sleep, and it's cold."

"It ain't like Vermont winter," Ames said. "Lord, it was seventeen below at my barn this morning."

"It's cold enough," Gracie insisted. "I saw this old woman on TV last night. They showed her hands. She was kinda holding them tight like this"—Gracie clutched her hands together in front of her ample bosom—"and she didn't have any gloves. She was just holding onto herself and shivering. It killed me. I couldn't sleep last night thinking about that poor old woman."

I thought Gracie was going to burst into tears, but she pulled herself together enough to get me a huge steaming plate of meat loaf, mashed potatoes, and beans, with three hot rolls on the side. She knows how I love her rolls.

Just then I felt a blast of air on my back. We all turned to look at the door. A man was standing there —a stranger. There was several days' growth of stubble on his face. He had on worn jeans and a flimsy baseball jacket and no hat or gloves. He was not anyone from around here.

"Take a seat," Gracie said. "Be right with you." Before I could ask for the ketchup, she was back to the Armenians. "And those children. Did you see those poor kids in the hospital with their legs all crushed? One little boy couldn't even remember who he was. The doctor didn't know if his parents were dead or alive."

I opened my mouth during the pause to ask for the ketchup, but by then she had turned to the stranger. "Now, what can I do for you?" she asked.

He was still standing in front of the door as though he couldn't remember what he'd come in for. "Coffee," he muttered at last. "To go."

"People who got through the earthquake are just freezing to death from the cold," Gracie went on as she filled a large Styrofoam cup from the coffee urn.

The man looked puzzled. "Armenians," I said. "She's all upset about the Armenians."

It was obvious he didn't know what we were talking about. "There was a big earthquake over there. They think about fifty to sixty thousand people died."

"And the rest are likely to." Gracie gave a huge

sigh. "Right at Christmas. I can't get over those poor children. Cream and sugar?"

"Yeah," the man said. "Both. Double."

Gracie put two teaspoons of sugar and a huge dollop of cream into the cup and pushed on a lid. "That'll be sixty-three cents," she said as the man handed her a dollar bill. "This mason jar here is for the Armenians," she said, pointing to it. "I'm taking donations—if you'd like to put in your change . . ."

The man took the change she held out and stuffed it into the pocket of his jeans. "How far to Burlington from here?" he asked.

"Well," said Gracie—you could tell she was a little bit annoyed that the man didn't care anything about her Armenians—"you get back on the interstate, it's about forty miles."

"I just came from there," I said, sticking my two cents in like a fool. "Road's terrible."

"Ah, they'll plow soon," said Ewell.

"I need gas," the man said.

"Well, that might be more of a problem. Nothing open this time of night," Ames said.

The man shrugged. He looked at Gracie, but she ignored him, carefully refilling my water glass. "Ben," she said. "You feeling lonely in that big place, come have Christmas dinner here with me."

"Thanks, Gracie," I said, keeping my back to the stranger. "I just might."

I felt the cold air as he opened the door to go. He muttered something as he went out. It sounded like "Damned Armenians," but maybe I just imagined that.

"Friendly soul," Ewell remarked.

"Not too worried about your Russians, either," Ames teased.

"Armenians," Gracie said looking sadder than ever, so when I was ready to go I stuffed all my change into the jar, even though I'd given her a twenty.

The first thing I did when I got back home was to hang out the NO VACANCY sign. I wasn't likely to get any visitors on a night like this, but I wasn't taking any chances. I had the evening all planned: first a roaring fire in the woodstove, then a large bottle of Coke and a two-pound bag of potato chips, then three rented videos in a row, none of which I would have been able to watch had there been anyone else in the house.

I had no sooner popped the first tape into the machine and settled back to watch when the doorbell rang . . . and rang . . . and rang. There was nothing to do but go answer. I put on the chain and opened the door a crack. "Sorry, no vacancy," I said, and then I saw it was the stranger from Gracie's.

"How about if I just stay in the garage?" he asked. "Like you said, the interstate is terrible, and it's freezing out here in the car."

It wasn't my problem. "Sorry," I said. "No vacancies. There's Woodley's just off the interstate."

"I already tried there," he said. "I ain't got sixty-five dollars."

"Well, if I could let you stay, which I can't, it's sixty-five here, too."

"Look, I'm just asking to stay in your garage, so I won't freeze to death. You'd let a stray dog into the garage, wouldn't you, night like this?"

I hesitated. I didn't really like his looks. Besides, the Pontiac was in there. If anything happened to that car, my mother would kill me.

He smiled then—the kind of shifty-eyed smile that immediately makes you distrust someone. "Just think of me as one of them Armenians," he said.

He was right. Fake smile or not, he *would* freeze to death in his car on a night like this. "Okay," I said. "Wait. I'll have to get my car out to make room for yours." I closed the front door and carefully locked it before going out through the kitchen to the attached garage. I got in the 4 x 4, pushed the button for the electric door, and slowly backed out. A ten-year-old Chevrolet with rusted sides drove into the slot beside the Pontiac. I got the old blankets out of the cargo area, then locked the 4 x 4 and hurried into the garage.

I put the blankets on the back of the Chevy. "Here's some blankets in case," I yelled as I pushed the button to close the door. I couldn't look at his old car. I couldn't think of the man out here when I had a roaring fire going in the kitchen. But I sure wasn't going to let him inside. People get robbed and beaten up for that kind of stupidity—murdered, even.

He didn't say anything, not even thanks. But it didn't matter. I gave him what he asked for—more than he asked for.

I went in and turned up the VCR very loud. . . . I don't know how long the knocking had been going on before I finally heard it. "Yeah?" I yelled through the closed kitchen door.

"Daddy said, could I use the bathroom?"

I was so startled to hear a kid's voice, I opened the door. Sure enough, there stood a dirty, skinny, red-faced kid. "Daddy said you'd let me use the bathroom."

I just opened the door wider and let him in. What

was I supposed to do? Tell the kid to go out in the snow? Sheesh. I shut the door behind him and led him to the downstairs powder room. "Don't use the towels," I warned.

I waited outside the bathroom for what seemed like ten minutes. What in the world was the kid up to? Finally, he came out, walking tall and straight backed like some little prince. He didn't say a word, not even thank you.

"You're welcome," I said loudly as I let him out the door, but he didn't look my way.

I just sat down. The guy hadn't said anything about any kid. I was sure he hadn't. I probably should call the welfare people or the police or somebody. I hadn't figured out what to do when there was another, softer knock on the kitchen door.

This time I just opened it. "You've been to the bathroom already," I started to say when I saw it was a different kid—a stringy-haired little girl with a runny nose rubbed raw. "Where did you come from?" I asked.

She whispered something.

"What?"

Again, I caught the word *bathroom*, so I shut the door and pointed her to the powder room. I didn't even bother to warn her about my mother's fancy guest towels. Somehow, I knew this was going to be a long night.

Before the kid had left the bathroom, there was another knock. I snatched open the door, all ready to give the guy a piece of my mind. But this time a woman stood there, holding a baby in a filthy rag of a blanket.

I couldn't believe it. This was like one of those circus acts where people just keep coming out of a car. "Would you warm it?" she asked. I looked down. She was handing me a baby bottle. It was about half full of frozen milk.

"You better do it," I said. I got her a saucepan, filled it with water, and turned on the burner. "The kid—the little girl's in the bathroom," I said, nodding in that direction. I waited, as patiently as I could, for the woman to test the milk on her wrist and shove the bottle into the baby's mouth, and for the little girl to finish wiping her grubby little hands on all four of Mom's embroidered Irish linen guest towels.

"Now," I said. "I'm very sorry, but you're going to have to go."

"It's cold out there," the little girl whined as I tried to gently urge her out the door.

"I know," I said grimly, going out with her around the Pontiac toward the Chevy. The man was sitting there behind the wheel, with all the windows rolled up. I went to the driver's side and tapped, but he didn't roll the window down. He looked straight ahead. I banged louder. "You're going to have to go," I said. "This isn't going to work. You didn't tell me you had kids with you."

The man turned slowly and opened the window a crack. He gave me a look—it was the most sarcastic expression I've ever seen on a man's face. "Just pretend we're some of them Armenians," he said and rolled the window up again.

I stood there for a minute, trying to figure out what to do next. It was so quiet I could hear the soft sounds of the baby drinking its milk. The little girl was watching me from the other side of the Chevy with big scared eyes. The woman hadn't moved. She was still standing in the doorway, the baby cradled in her arms, a dark silhouette against the light streaming from the bright kitchen. ". . . 'Round yon Virgin Mother and Child . . ." A shiver went through me.

"I'm sorry," I said to her, and I really was. It wasn't her fault. "I'm sorry, but you're going to have to find someplace else. I don't own this place. I'm just taking care of it, and the owners wouldn't approve of me letting people stay in the garage."

No one moved, but the little girl began to whimper again.

"I think there's a shelter or something in Barre. I could call on the phone . . ." Still no one moved.

I went back to the kitchen door and pressed the opener button on the wall.. The garage light flashed on and the door rattled up. The woman jumped, and the little girl started crying in earnest. "I'm sorry," I said again, although I was beginning to feel more angry than sorry. That jerk had really taken advantage.

Just pretend we're some of them Armenians. The nerve. I watched the woman help the crying child into the backseat of the car and climb in after her. The baby's blanket caught on something and she jerked it free. I could hear a tearing sound. At the front window the boy sat, his nose flattened against the pane.

I waited but nothing happened. The man was just going to sit there. Anger washed away what guilt I might have felt. I went around to the man's window again. "If you don't move out of here," I said, "I'm calling the police."

The man acted as if he hadn't heard. Suppose he just stayed there and they all froze to death right in our garage? Imagine the headlines—NO ROOM IN THE INN: HOMELESS FAMILY FREEZES AT LOCAL B & B. "I'm not kidding," I shouted. "I'm calling the cops!"

Through the closed windows of the Chevy, I could hear the little girl crying. "Come on!" I yelled to block out the sound. "Get outta here!"

Finally, he started the motor and began to back out slowly. I ran to the 4 x 4. As soon as the Chevy was out of the way, I was going to drive it in and close the door. The snow had stopped. The plows would be out soon. They'd be okay. An unheated barn was no place for a baby.

And then I heard myself. "Away in a manger, no crib for his bed." No room in the inn, not for two thousand lousy years. Never.

The Chevy had stalled in the driveway. I jumped out and ran to the driver's window and pounded on it again. He stopped grinding the starter and turned to give me his sarcastic look. "We're going," he said.

"I changed my mind."

Now he opened the window. "What you say?"

"Put your car back in and come on in the house. It's freezing out here."

He smiled grimly. "Thinking about them Armenians, huh?"

"No," I said. "Actually, I was thinking about something else."

I led the way into the kitchen and found them chairs so they could sit around the stove and get warm. Then I went to the phone to call Gracie. I knew I needed help, and she was sure to come. I'd just tell her I had a houseful of Armenians.

About the Author

Katherine Paterson was born in China, the daughter of missionary parents. Educated in both China and the United States, she graduated from King College in Bristol, Tennessee, and received a master's degree from the Presbyterian School of Christian Education in Richmond, Virginia. After studying and working in Japan for four years, she was awarded a fellowship to Union Theological Seminary in New York City, where she met her husband, the Reverend John B. Paterson. The Patersons have four grown children and two grandchildren and live in Barre, Vermont.

A two-time recipient of both the Newbery Medal and National Book Award for her novels, Katherine

Paterson has also published essays and written a book in collaboration with her husband. A previous collection of Christmas stories, *Angels and Other Strangers*, was published by Crowell (now HarperCollins) in 1979.